WE HAVE A DEAD GOLDFISH ON OUR HANDS.

By now, of course, Alfie is sobbing—like that's going to help Zip. Or me. "I wanted him to have a *pa-a-arty*," she wails. "I felt sorry for him! And I thought if I fed him all at once, I wouldn't have to do it anymore from now on. I could just *play* with him."

"Well, congratulations," I tell her. "Because now, *no one* has to feed him. He's dead forever! And what am I supposed to tell Ms. Sanchez next Monday? 'Sorry I killed the brand-new pet that your boyfriend won for you at the church festival, but I couldn't keep the goldfish alive even for a *week*?' How is that gonna make me look, did you ever think of that, Alfie? Huh? Everyone in my class is going to hate me!"

OTHER BOOKS YOU MAY ENJOY

EllRay Jakes
walks the plank!

BY **Sally Warner**

ILLUSTRATED BY
Jamie Harper

PUFFIN BOOKS
An Imprint of Penguin Group (USA) Inc.

PUFFIN BOOKS

Published by the Penguin Group

Penguin Young Readers Group, 345 Hudson Street, New York, New York 10014, U.S.A.

Penguin Group (Canada), 90 Eglinton Avenue East, Suite 700, Toronto, Ontario, Canada M4P 2Y3
(a division of Pearson Penguin Canada Inc.)

Penguin Books Ltd, 80 Strand, London WC2R 0RL, England

Penguin Ireland, 25 St Stephen's Green, Dublin 2, Ireland (a division of Penguin Books Ltd)

Penguin Group (Australia), 250 Camberwell Road, Camberwell, Victoria 3124, Australia
(a division of Pearson Australia Group Pty Ltd)

Penguin Books India Pvt Ltd, 11 Community Centre, Panchsheel Park, New Delhi - 110 017, India

Penguin Group (NZ), 67 Apollo Drive, Rosedale, Auckland 0632, New Zealand
(a division of Pearson New Zealand Ltd.)

Penguin Books (South Africa) (Pty) Ltd, 24 Sturdee Avenue,
Rosebank, Johannesburg 2196, South Africa

Penguin Books Ltd, Registered Offices: 80 Strand, London WC2R 0RL, England

First published in the United States of America by Viking,
a division of Penguin Young Readers Group, 2012
Published by Puffin Books, a member of Penguin Young Readers Group, 2013

15 17 19 20 18 16 14

THE LIBRARY OF CONGRESS HAS CATALOGED THE VIKING EDITION AS FOLLOWS:

Warner, Sally.

EllRay Jakes walks the plank / by Sally Warner ; illustrated by Jamie Harper.

p. cm.

Summary: Third-grader EllRay is becoming famous for messing up when his
little sister accidentally kills the classroom goldfish EllRay is taking care of
and then he leaves his teacher's read-aloud book at home.

ISBN 978-0-670-06306-2 (hardcover)

[1. Behavior—Fiction. 2. Responsibility—Fiction. 3. Schools—Fiction.
4. African Americans—Fiction.]
I. Harper, Jamie, ill. II. Title.

PZ7.W24644Ep 2012   [Fic]—dc23   2011016029

Puffin Books ISBN 978-0-14-242409-4

Book design by Nancy Brennan
Text set in ITC Century

Printed in the United States of America

ALWAYS LEARNING   PEARSON

For Lucy and Noah Parsons —S.W.
For Alison and Maddie —J.H.

CONTENTS

X X X

EllRay Jakes
walks the plank!

* 1 *

ZIP, NOT SWIMMY

"Why do you hate Swimmy?" my four-year-old sister Alfie asks me one rainy afternoon in April during spring break.

"I don't hate him," I say, pressing PAUSE on my hand-held video game. And it's true. I just don't want to start liking him too much, that's all. He has to go back to school on Monday.

Alfie and I are both sitting on my bed, but I am the only one who is supposed to be here. I was alone in my room, leaning against my pillows minding my own business, trying to top my personal best in *Die, Creature, Die*. Mom thinks the game is too violent, but it's not. It's just space creatures you are socking with your **FIST OF DOOM**. But Alfie ruined the whole thing.

"He's just a regular goldfish," I say. "He's barely

even two inches long. What is there to hate?"

"But you don't *like* him," Alfie says, not backing down.

Everyone says how cute my sister is, but they don't know how stubborn she can be. She is golden-brown like an acorn, and she has big brown eyes. She  usually wears her hair in three puffy little braids, one on each side of her head and one sort of in the back. It's hard to explain girls' hair right.

I am *so* glad I do not have to be the one to fix Alfie's hair each morning, by the way! You should hear the yelling. And Alfie's braids have to be just perfect. I feel sorry for my mom.

"That fish is not even ours, Alfie," I remind her—and I remind myself, because I secretly really do like him. He is very unusual for a goldfish. He has a white spot on his stomach, and you can just tell how smart he is. Also, I think he knows me now. "And his name's Zip, not Swimmy," I remind Alfie.

"You'll just confuse him if you start calling him by the wrong name."

Zip is actually Ms. Sanchez's goldfish, and Ms. Sanchez is my third grade teacher at Oak Glen Primary School, in Oak Glen, California. Oak Glen is about an hour away from San Diego if the traffic is bad, which my dad says it always is.

Ms. Sanchez's boyfriend won Zip for her at a church festival two weeks ago when he tossed a ping-pong ball into a bowl of water the size of a softball. Ms. Sanchez says this is a lot harder to do than it looks.

And then Ms. Sanchez brought her new fish to our classroom so it wouldn't be alone all day. She says Zip will be our class mascot, and that having an official pet will also "help remind us of other living things."

I think there are plenty of "other living things" in our class already, like fifteen girls and ten boys, only *ten*, and I am reminded of them every single day.

But whatever!

When it was time for our school's spring break, I volunteered to take care of Zip at my house for the whole week. Ms. Sanchez was going to fly to Texas to see her family, but *my* family wasn't going anywhere, because our dad had geology classes to teach at a college in San Diego.

Our family's vacations almost never come out even, except in the summer.

A goldfish is probably the only thing in the whole universe Alfie isn't allergic to, so this was going to be my big chance to see what it was like having a pet in the house. And I was happy to volunteer to take care of Zip, because I kind of felt sorry for him, not getting to go to Texas with Ms. Sanchez just because he's a fish.

He can't help that.

Maybe I'll get extra credit from Ms. Sanchez for taking such good care of her new pet, our class mascot. I could use some extra credit, that's for sure.

My name is EllRay Jakes, and I am eight years old, and I am having the worst semester *EVER*.

But that means things can only get better, right?

TWO SHAKES

Since we can't go on vacation, my mom got the idea of "taking a vacation at home." So far . . . it has been pretty fun, I have to admit. Here is how we've spent our time.

1. Alfie and I take turns choosing what cartoon show to watch in the morning, which means that every other morning we get to watch something good.

2. Also, we have been on a couple of picnics with Mom, and two hikes, until Alfie complained that her feet were too short to hike any more. Ever again.

3. And we went to see a movie one afternoon, but it was for four-year-olds like Alfie, not eight-

year-olds like me. The popcorn was good, though.

4. We even went to the San Diego Zoo one day, and then we surprised my dad by visiting his office at the college. It really was a surprise for him, too! And when my mom went to get a cup of coffee, Alfie sat on the office photocopy machine and copied her own rear end. Luckily, she was wearing shorts at the time. And then I dropped a giant box of paper-clips on my dad's office floor, and they went everywhere.

5. Dad said he had a meeting pretty soon after that, so Mom and Alfie and I went home.

"Swimmy is confused already, *EllWay*," Alfie tells me, pronouncing my name wrong, as usual. "And I *like* the name Swimmy. It's in my favorite book by Leo Lionni. And our family should be the ones who get to name him, because we're the ones who decorated his fish house."

This part of her crazy explanation is actually

true. Ms. Sanchez already bought Zip a bigger bowl, because his old softball-sized one was so small, and Zip was growing. My mom is the one who bought him a castle to swim through.

Mom writes fantasy books for grown-ups. That's why she loves castles. And that's also why Alfie and I have such weird names: "Alfleta," which means "beautiful elf" in old Saxon, which no one even speaks anymore, probably not even old Saxons, and "Lancelot Raymond" for me. Lancelot was a guy in a famous old story.

L-period-Ray. EllRay. Get it?

And yes, a substitute teacher did say my real name out loud in class once last fall, and it was a disaster—especially because I'm the shortest kid in Ms. Sanchez's third grade class, even counting the girls. So how could I fight back when kids started teasing me? Especially the sometimes-mean ones like Jared Matthews and Cynthia Harbison?

But getting back to Zip, even Dad got interested in fixing up his new bowl. He gave me half a geode to make the whole place sparkle.

A geode is like a trick rock, and it's one of the coolest things in the world. All geodes are round, gray, and boring on the outside, but if you cut them in half with a special saw, there are beautiful crystals growing inside where the hollow part is.

It's like there's a surprise present inside each one.

So now Zip's sparkly geode sits right next to Mom's castle, but Zip doesn't even seem to notice it. I guess he misses Ms. Sanchez too much, or maybe he's still mad about Texas.

But Zip does care about food, and that's where I come in. Feeding him is my job this spring break. I give him two shakes of goldfish food first thing in the morning and two more shakes of food just before bed.

I have to admit it's not as much fun as I thought it would be.

"Call him whatever you want to, Alfie. I don't care," I tell my little sister, giving up. "You're not the one who has to feed him. I'm the one doing all the work around here."

"I could feed him for the rest of the week," Alfie says, excited.

"Nuh-uh," I say, turning back to my video game. "It's way too hard."

"Please?" Alfie asks, and her face crinkles up.

Uh-oh. This is a bad sign with her. It's the crying sign.

"PLEASE?" she begs.

"Well," I say, giving in, "maybe just at night. But I'll have to show you how."

"I know how," she says. "I've been watching you."

"Just two shakes," I remind her.

"Just two shakes. And I only get to do it at night," she repeats, so happy that she even makes *me* smile—which I am also doing because I have accidentally tricked her into doing one of my chores.

"So, I'll see you later," I say, hoping she'll take the hint and scram.

"Okay," Alfie says, hopping off my bed. "See you at supper. Bye, EllWay!"

That was easy, I think, getting back to my game's space creatures and their terrible fate.

What could go wrong?

✱ **3** ✱

A DISASTER

The first thing I see the next morning is the last thing I ever wanted to see.

It's Zip, and he's not zippy *or* swimmy. He's floating.

Not in a fun way, either.

He is on his side, and he is surrounded by gummy brown fish food that is all stuck together. The fish food covers the entire surface of the water in Ms. Sanchez's newly decorated bowl, which is sitting on my desk.

Zip is dead.

Zip, with the white spot on his stomach.

Zip, who was smart, you could just tell.

Zip, who knew me.

Zip, who was counting on me to take good care of him.

What happened?

Alfie. That's what happened. This is a disaster.

"Alfie," I shout. "*Alfie!* Come in here right now and see what you did!"

Instead of Alfie, Mom comes rushing into my room. "EllRay, what in the world is going on?" she asks. "Alfie is brushing her teeth." And then she sees the fish bowl—and what is floating in it.

Zip is so dead that he practically has little Xs where his eyes are, like in the cartoons.

"Oh, my," Mom says, covering her mouth with her hand. "And this *would* be the morning your father left early to go to the gym."

"Alfie murdered Zip," I say, in case Mom has missed seeing the empty fish food container lying next to the bowl. "She *fed* him to death. She begged and begged me to let her help, and I finally said yes, but I told her *two shakes*. And look what she did!"

Alfie trots into my room, her pink toothbrush

drooping in her hand. "What's the matter, EllWay?" she asks.

"A dead goldfish, that's what's the *matter*, Einstein," I tell her, pointing.

PLONK goes her goopy toothbrush onto my floor. "Swimmy!" Alfie cries, throwing herself against the bowl and hugging it with both arms.

"His name's Zip!" I say, shouting again. "At least it *was*. What did you do?"

By now, of course, Alfie is sobbing—like that's going to help Zip. Or me. "I wanted him to have a *pa-a-arty*," she wails. "I felt sorry for him! And I

thought if I fed him all at once, I wouldn't have to do it anymore from now on. I could just *play* with him."

"Well, congratulations," I tell her. "Because now, *no one* has to feed him. He's dead forever!

And what am I supposed to tell Ms. Sanchez next Monday? 'Sorry I killed the brand-new pet that your boyfriend won for you at the church festival, but I couldn't keep a goldfish alive even for a *week*?' How is that gonna make me look, did you ever think of that, Alfie? Huh? Everyone in my class is going to hate me!"

"Who cares how it makes you look?" Alfie yells back at me, tears spurting out of her eyes. "Think about Swimmy!"

4

DEAD OR ALIVE

"Hang on, you two," Mom tells us. "Let's focus. We've got a dead goldfish on our hands, here."

"He had a name, Mom. *Zip*. And this is all Alfie's fault," I say.

"I'm only four!"

"But you dumped the whole container of fish food into the bowl," I remind her. "After you promised you'd do it right!"

"Didn't you notice all that food floating in the bowl last night, EllRay?" Mom asks me. "Before you turned out the light?"

"No. I didn't even look," I say. "I was trying to finish *Treasure Island*, that book Ms. Sanchez let me take home over vacation. Why, are you saying I should have checked to make sure Zip wasn't eating his head off? Or maybe even flying around the room?"

"I don't think eating too much killed him," Mom says, looking into the fish bowl once more. "He probably choked from all that food clogging up his poor little gills."

"Oh, *that's* better," I say. "Thanks for telling me, Mom."

"Look," my mother says, frowning. "I know you're upset, EllRay, and this is definitely a bad morning for all of us. But let's not get snippy. That's not going to help the situation or change anything."

"But what are we going to do?" I ask.

"Bury him," Mom says. "Or flush him, if it's too rainy to go outside and dig a hole. I mean a grave."

"Flush him down the toilet? Like *poo*?" Alfie asks, completely grossed out by now, on top of being sad.

"We are not flushing him," I say. "I should bring him back to Ms. Sanchez, dead or alive. Because I have to prove what happened, don't I? He's *evidence*. Otherwise, people might think I just decided to keep him. And we don't even know what religion Ms. Sanchez is, Mom. Maybe she'll want to bury him at her own church."

"No, *we* get to bury him," Alfie says, frowning. "And I'll say a little prayer."

"I suppose we could put him in the refrigerator until Monday," Mom says, trying to think fast.

"No!" Alfie and I yell at the exact same time. The thought of Zip's poor little orange dead body lying next to Mom's low-fat peach yogurt is just too much.

"I'd wrap him up first," Mom says, trying to calm

us down. "And put him in two or three thick plastic bags. Or maybe he could go into the freezer," she says to herself, as if that would be a whole lot better.

"Next to the *ice cream*?" Alfie asks, horrified.

"We're out of ice cream," Mom reminds her.

"Next to where the ice cream is supposed to be?" Alfie says, looking even more upset than before, as if this might ruin ice cream for her forever.

"What a **DISASTER**," I say—to myself, not to my mom or my little sister.

"We could buy Ms. Sanchez another fish," Mom suggests.

"You mean *trick* her?" I say, surprised that my mother would come up with a sneaky plan like this one.

Besides, I already figured out that trying to fool Ms. Sanchez would never work. What about that spot on his stomach? And the intelligent expression on his face?

"Not *trick* her," Mom says. "We'll call her first, and we'll tell her what happened. Then we'll offer to buy her another goldfish just as nice. We could ask about the—the disposal of the remains at the same time, I guess."

"What are 'remains'?" Alfie asks, sounding suspicious.

"She means his body," I tell my sister. "His *dead body*, Alfie."

"EllRay," Mom says in a warning voice.

"Well, excuse me," I say. "But Ms. Sanchez happens to be in Texas. And I'm the one who's going to suffer for this, Mom, since Zip is d-e-a-d *dead*. How do you think I'm going to feel walking into class next Monday with an empty fish bowl in my arms?"

"But we get to keep the castle," Alfie says, like that's a well-known fact. "And the sparkle rock, too."

"It's called a geode, and no, we don't," I tell her, almost glad to say something that will make her feel sad. "They belong to Ms. Sanchez and her next goldfish, who I'll probably never even be allowed to *meet*, in case he faints or even drops dead when he sees me."

"Mommy!" Alfie yelps.

"Downstairs, the both of you," Mom says, sounding strict. "EllRay, pour your little sister a nice bowl of crunchy cereal and a cold glass of juice. I've got some cleaning up to do in here," she adds, trying to hide her shudder as she peeks at poor Zip, who is floating like a little orange island in a muddy brown lake.

It is obvious that Alfie doesn't want to go downstairs and miss out on all the gory drama. "But Mommy, I—"

"C'mon, Alfie," I say. "I'll let you choose the cartoon this morning, even if it's the one about those princess kittens."

"Thanks, EllRay," my mom calls out as we leave the room.

"It's my day to choose the cartoon anyway," Alfie says over her shoulder.

"Whatever," I tell her, sighing. "What-*ever*."

✳ **5** ✳

INVISIBLE PET DAY

It is now Monday morning, and spring break is over, and it has finally stopped raining. But everything is still shiny outside as I walk up Oak Glen Primary School's front steps, being careful not to spill the water in Ms. Sanchez's goldfish bowl.

No, there's no fish inside the bowl, because when she got back from Texas, Ms. Sanchez told my mom she'd rather wait a while before buying a new one. But I wanted the kids in my class to see the castle and the geode, at least, so they'd know how hard I tried to make Zip happy while they were away on their fun vacation trips. And since I didn't want the castle and geode clanking around inside an empty bowl, I filled it with water before I left home, even though my mom said that was inviting disaster.

Too late, Mom! Disaster already came.

"Mr. Jakes," the principal calls out with a big smile on his face—I *think*. It's hard to tell with that beard. He walks down a couple of steps to greet me. He likes to say hi to kids in the morning, especially the ones he knows.

This includes me, but that's another story. Okay, two stories.

"Did you have a nice vacation?" the principal asks as I stand on the step, trying not to let any water slosh out of the bowl when other kids push by.

"It was okay," I say, being polite. "Did you have a nice vacation too?"

"Sure did," he says, and then he peers into the bowl. "Hmm," he says. "Did someone forget to tell me it's **INVISIBLE PET DAY** here at Oak Glen?"

This is his idea of a joke, I guess.

"Nope," I say. "I'm just returning Ms. Sanchez's fish bowl. I was taking care of it for her while she was in Texas."

"Well, that was nice of you," he says, waiting for the rest of the story.

Emma McGraw and Annie Pat Masterson are coming up the stairs on my right, I see, wishing I could disappear before they see me. They are whispering and giggling together, so maybe they won't notice me standing here with a basically empty fish bowl in my arms, talking to our principal, who is probably the tallest bearded man in the world.

Yeah, right. I don't stand out at all!

"EllRay," Annie Pat says, screeching to a halt. "Where's Zip?"

Just my luck. She wants to be a marine biologist when she grows up, so naturally she'd notice something like a missing fish.

"He decided to walk to school today," I say, but when Annie Pat and Emma jump back and start examining the concrete steps as if Zip might be trying to climb them one at a time, I realize it didn't sound as funny as I hoped.

"I'm just kidding," I tell them. I hate it when I have to explain a joke.

"But where is he?" Emma asks, her eyes wide.

"Ms. Sanchez will tell you," I say. "She said she'd make an announcement."

✕ ✕ ✕

"And so I know we're all very sad," our teacher says, shortly after taking attendance and announcing the death of Zip Sanchez, not naming the actual murderer. "But these things happen, and life goes on. Any questions?"

Everyone stares at Zip's empty bowl, which is sitting on the table behind Ms. Sanchez's desk.

She just loved the castle and the geode, by the way.

Ms. Sanchez is the prettiest teacher in our whole school. I only hope her boyfriend doesn't get too mad about me killing the prize he won for her. He's *huge*!

Slowly, slowly, Heather Patton's hand goes up. Heather wears her hair pulled back tight in a ponytail, and she likes everything to be perfect, and she says she's allergic to coconut, but who knows? Another thing about Heather is that she kisses up to Cynthia Harbison all the time. Cynthia is the bossiest girl in our class, and that's saying something.

"Yes, Heather?" Ms. Sanchez asks, looking surprised. I guess she didn't really expect there to *be* any questions, because—what is there to say?

Dead is dead.

"Is Zip in heaven?" Heather asks.

The second Heather says this, Ms. Sanchez looks like she just got hit with a water balloon. And

then kids start to **BUZZ-BUZZ-BUZZ** all around me, and a bunch of hands shoot up high in the air.

Jared Matthews, Stanley Washington, Fiona McNulty, Kry Rodriguez, Annie Pat, Emma, Cynthia, and my friends Corey Robinson and Kevin McKinley all have their hands up. It looks like lots of kids have an opinion about whether or not Zip has made it up to heaven.

"I—I'm afraid we'll have to talk about pets and the afterlife at some future time," Ms. Sanchez says, stumbling over the words. "Because we have a lot of work to catch up on, ladies and gentlemen. So let's take a look at our spelling words for the week, shall we?"

And slowly, slowly, the hands go down.

✳ 6 ✳

NUTRITION BREAK

"What happened?" Emma and Annie Pat ask me first thing during nutrition break—which at Oak Glen Primary School is morning recess with healthy snacks.

Supposedly healthy snacks.

We're also supposed to get what Ms. Sanchez calls "fresh air and exercise" during nutrition break, which is why we have it outside on the playground, with kick balls and everything. But today, even though we are all outside, I don't think we'll be getting much exercise *or* nutrition.

Jared is chewing strips of red licorice, and Fiona is eating barbecue-flavored corn chips. Stanley is sharing a box of leftover yellow Peeps with Corey, and Kry is dipping her hand into a little bag of plain chocolate chips, which she likes to eat without any cookie involved. She says it's quicker that way.

And *all* the third-graders in my class, even the ones who happen to be eating healthy snacks, are gathered in front of me as I lean against the icy cold chain-link fence.

My stomach is gurgling like crazy for its own morning snack, which today is little sandwiches made from saltine crackers with almond butter glue holding them together, since it's "No Peanuts!" at our school in case of allergies, which some kids have. But I guess I won't get a chance to eat my crackers, not with all the explaining I have to do.

One thing for sure, I have decided not to tell anyone Alfie was the one who accidentally killed Zip. She feels bad enough already. I will take the blame.

Alfie's my little sister, no matter what.

"What happened is that the lid came off the fish food container while I was shaking out the food," I tell Emma and Annie Pat, making up the lie on the spot. "And it all dumped in at once. And there was nothing I could do, because Zip died instantly. And *painlessly*," I add, hoping this will make everyone feel better.

Annie Pat shakes her head, and when she does,

her twin red pigtails shake too. "But I have an aquarium at home," she says. "And the fish food lid does not come off that easily."

"And anyway," Emma says, frowning, "the whole story doesn't make any sense. I'm not saying you're a liar, EllRay. You must have forgotten some of the details, that's all. Zip would not have died instantly. So why didn't you take him out of the bowl and give him CPR, and then clean everything up and start over?"

Emma and I are almost friends, and so I know that she is not trying to make me look bad. She just wants to know what happened, that's all.

Emma's like that.

Forty-two eyes—three kids are absent today—stare hard at me as I try to ooze backward through the chain-link fence. "I'm just saying what happened," I tell everyone, wishing I was anyplace else but here—even at the doctor's, about to get a shot.

And that's my worst thing. "I can't help it if your fish food jar is different from Ms. Sanchez's," I say to Annie Pat. "She's the one who bought it."

"Well, I guess I believe EllRay," my friend Kevin says slowly, as if he's had to give it a lot of thought.

"Yeah," Corey says. "No matter what really happened."

Thanks a lot, guys.

Cynthia flips up the collar on her fuzzy red jacket and shrugs. "Well, who cares what happened, or how it happened?" she asks. "It was only a goldfish."

"Yeah. We're sorry for Ms. Sanchez and everything, but it *was*," her friend Heather chimes in, trying to be loyal to Cynthia but nice to our teacher at the same time. Heather wants everyone to like her.

Good luck with that, by the way.

"My neighbor has a fish called an oscar in his aquarium," Jared says, his gums and tongue all red from the licorice. "And it *eats* goldfish. My neighbor buys 'em ten at a time! He calls them 'feeder fish,' and he doesn't even give them names. So what's the big deal about one dead goldfish, even if it was a prize?"

"That's so sad that the poor little things don't even get to have names," Fiona says, ignoring the part about how the other fish eats them. She's got that orange dust they put on barbecue chips all around her mouth.

"Eww. A cannibal fish named Oscar. Gross," Cynthia and Heather say with twin squeals, but Annie Pat looks interested. Remember, she's the one who wants to be a marine biologist when she grows up.

"Is it a tiger oscar?" she asks, her dark blue eyes shining with excitement. "They live in the Amazon River, in South America."

"I'm never swimming *there*," Cynthia says to Heather, and Heather nods her head in agreement.

Heather always sides with Cynthia. I think she's scared not to.

I can't help but feel a little happy that this terrible conversation has moved so far away from what a mess-up I am for supposedly killing Zip, our new class mascot, Ms. Sanchez's prize goldfish. In fact, the talk has moved all the way from Oak Glen, California, to the Amazon River, in South America. That's pretty far! Maybe I'll get a chance to eat a cracker or two after all. I start to relax.

"Where did you bury Zip, EllRay?" Kry asks, after popping another chocolate chip into her mouth.

And—**WHOOSH**, we're back in Oak Glen with a dead fish.

"In my backyard," I say, trying to look serious and sad at the same time.

Don't tell anyone, but really, Zip's funeral was a little bit funny. Here is what happened.

1. It was still raining the morning when we buried him, but we each had an umbrella. Well, everyone except Zip.

2. And we couldn't find a little box to put him in, so Alfie stretched Zip out on a blue plastic doll bed from this set she has. Then she covered him with a Kleenex pretend-blanket, and she put an ivy leaf over his face so she wouldn't have to look at it again, because that was the part of Zip that looked the most dead. The rest of him almost looked okay.

3. Then Mom put Zip and the bed into a plastic

container—like he was some really weird leftover.

4. Then I dug a muddy hole in the backyard with Mom's small gardening shovel.

5. And then we put the plastic container in the hole, and my mom said some nice stuff about Zip, even though she barely knew him.

6. Then Alfie said her prayer, only it got so long that Mom had to say "Amen!" just to give Alfie an excuse to stop talking. Or to shut her up, I don't know which.

7. I wanted to say something nice about Zip too, because after all, I was the one who really knew him—and who was responsible for him. But I didn't want to start crying, not that anyone would even have noticed with all the rain.

That last part about Zip's funeral wasn't funny, but the rest of it was. Kind of.

It's confusing how something can be sad and funny at the same time. Or funny and sad.

"Well," Cynthia says, smoothing back her already-smooth hair. "Remind me never to ask you to take care of anything, EllRay Jakes."

And Heather gives Cynthia an admiring grin. "Yeah," she agrees.

"Like I *would*," I say back to both of them.

But really, I don't blame Cynthia and Heather for saying what they did.

Zip was my job.

I wouldn't ask a mess-up like me to take care of anything, either.

7

AN EXTRA LITTLE VACATION

It is still Monday, and we just had afternoon recess. But we have all been ready to go home for about two hours, even Ms. Sanchez. You can tell. Some of the hair that she usually wears pulled back in a shiny black bun is falling down, and there is a blue ink mark on her chin.

A couple of the girls put bunches of little flowers from the playground ice plant in front of Zip's empty fish bowl after lunch—to honor him, I guess. But Zip didn't know what flowers are. He was a fish. And those flowers aren't helping our mood any, especially my mood.

"Ladies and gentlemen," Ms. Sanchez says just as we are getting ready to take our dreaded weekly spelling quiz, the one that is repeated on Friday. "The first day back at school after a vacation is always hard, and today has been no exception to that unwritten rule. It has also been a sad day for us all, for obvious reasons."

Half the kids in our class look at Zip's empty fish bowl and the purple ice plant flowers when she says this, and half the kids look at me. I don't look anywhere.

"So I have decided to toss out our schedule for the rest of the afternoon," Ms. Sanchez says, "and give us all a much-needed break. An extra little vacation—on *Treasure Island*."

Okay. Ms. Sanchez has been reading us this great book called *Treasure Island*, by Robert Louis Stevenson, on Friday afternoons. "I think it's the first pirate story for children there ever was," she told us before she started. And even though this book was written more than a hundred years ago, it's pretty cool. **VERY COOL**, in fact, although it is a hard book to read alone when you're only eight years old. It has been hard for me, anyway. But the thing about books is that you can skip over the hard parts and still get the idea.

Time changes when Ms. Sanchez starts to read to us, and we change, too.

1. Emma and Annie Pat chew on their knuckles during the scary parts, which so far is most of the book.
2. Fiona bites her lip and draws pictures of whatever Ms. Sanchez is reading. Fiona is the shyest kid in our class, but she's a really good artist.
3. Stanley closes his eyes, and Jared and Kevin look at nothing, but they tilt their heads like they are listening in on someone.
4. And even though some part of me notices the other kids, all I am really seeing is Jim Hawkins, the boy in the book.

I think Jim Hawkins is pretty much like me, only white. Well, *maybe* he's white. And he's a few years older than I am, and probably taller. Most kids are. But differences like that don't matter, not with books.

I really like *Treasure Island*.

In fact, I like it so much that I took it home over spring break, because aboard the ship *Hispaniola*, Jim Hawkins had just overheard Long John Silver—who was supposed to be the ship's cook—

say he was going to kill everyone on the ship who wasn't a secret pirate. I couldn't wait a whole week without knowing what was going to happen next, could I?

How was I supposed to sleep at night?

So I asked Ms. Sanchez in a quiet voice if I could borrow the book over vacation, and she said yes, which is why *Treasure Island* is now sitting on the chair next to my bed.

That's right. I forgot to bring *Treasure Island* back to school today.

I was kind of busy with a couple of other things, remember?

"Let's see. Where could that book be?" Ms. Sanchez says, thinking out loud as she searches her shelves.

Wriggling around, my class makes an excited rustling noise that sounds like the wind blowing through tree branches on a stormy day. Kids are silently high-fiving each other on this piece of surprise good luck: being read to on a Monday afternoon, instead of having to take a spelling test.

But of course I sit frozen in my seat.

"Where did I put that book?" Ms. Sanchez asks herself, tapping her chin with her solid gold pen.

And all of a sudden, she remembers. "Oh," she says, and she slides a quick glance in my direction—then looks away.

Don't tell, don't tell, I think as hard as I can, hoping the words will somehow jump into Ms. Sanchez's brain, because this would just be one bad thing too many for the kids in my class to forgive. Ever.

Even Kevin and Corey. They will be ashamed they know me.

Killing Zip, the class mascot, *and* messing up a surprise story time?

No way!

I feel like I am about to **WALK THE PLANK**.

I guess Ms. Sanchez gets my silent message, because she says, "Oh, dear. I must have left *Treasure Island* at home. Silly me. Sorry, everyone. I guess we'd better take that quiz after all. Just a short, fun version of it, though."

Thank you, Ms. Sanchez.

First, thanks for not telling anyone that Alfie killed Zip, and now, thanks for this.

"No, wait," Cynthia Harbison says, her eyes getting skinny as she goes back in time inside her head. "*Treasure Island* can't be at your house, Ms. Sanchez, because EllRay borrowed it. Don't you remember? Right before vacation?"

Then Cynthia actually smiles like she expects to be congratulated.

And all my good feelings crash down around my feet—because Ms. Sanchez might be willing to pretend-forget something to keep a kid from

being embarrassed in class, but she's not the type of person who would ever tell a lie. Not once someone else remembered the truth.

"Oh, yes," Ms. Sanchez says, sighing. "Do you happen to have it with you, EllRay?"

"Nope," I tell her—and everyone else. "Sorry."

"Well, that's okay," Ms. Sanchez says in her nicest voice. "In fact, it's perfectly understandable.

You had your hands full. Anyway, we're running too short on time to do the book justice."

"Yeah. *Now* we are," Jared Matthews mumbles, giving me a dirty look.

"Oh, man," Stanley says, looking like someone just stole his lunch.

Corey and Kevin stare at me, then look away, as if they are trying to remember why we are friends.

"But that means there's no time for a spelling quiz, either," Ms. Sanchez tells us, her voice bright. I guess by saying this, she thinks she's sort of giving everyone an invisible present to keep them from hating me.

"The buzzer's about to go off," Annie Pat says, sounding gloomy, and she puts her hands over her ears in advance. Annie Pat has very sensitive ears.

"Any second now," Ms. Sanchez agrees, aiming her tired-looking smile around the room. "So I want everyone to go home and get a good night's sleep—because tomorrow is another day. *Thank goodness.*"

* 8 *

THE NAME YOU GET

"Are you still mad at me, EllWay?" Alfie asks that
night at home, a doll in each of her hands. I am supposed to be keeping her company while she picks
up her room, but at the same time I am sitting on
her rug playing *Die, Creature, Die* again. I am still
trying to top my personal best—which is not very
good.

"Only a little mad," I tell her after pressing
PAUSE, and I lean back against her bed. "Mostly I'm
mad at *me*. You didn't mean to do anything wrong,
Alfie. You were trying to help, but you're just four."

"But why are you mad at *you*?" she asks, sinking down next to me.

"Because I should have made sure you fed him
right," I say.

"Yeah," she says, nodding, and relief spreads
across her round face like syrup on a pancake. "It

was your fault Swimmy died. You messed up, huh?"

"Yeah," I say. "I messed up."

"But I'm the one who got in trouble at day care today," she says, staring at one of her dolls as she combs its bright yellow hair with her fingers.

"I heard," I say.

Mom told me that Alfie got sent home with a note—which is *the* bad thing at her day care. Alfie got mad and told Suzette Monahan that she was going to die some day and maybe be buried in the

backyard in a plastic container. Or else flushed.

Alfie didn't say whose backyard Suzette might be buried in, but it didn't matter, Mom says. Suzette was already yelling for the day care teacher before Alfie even finished her sentence.

Suzette is sometimes Alfie's friend and sometimes her enemy, and she is always a pain, in my opinion. She came over to our house once to play, and she even tried bossing my mom around about the snack. Big mistake, Suzette. Our mom is not a pushover.

"I guess I said something bad to Suzette," Alfie admits, twisting the doll's yellow hair.

"Why?" I ask.

"I don't know," Alfie says. "I was thinking about Swimmy, and then Suzette put torn-up pieces of paper in my hair and kids laughed, so the words just jumped out of my mouth. And now Suzette says she gets to be the cutest one in day care."

"The cutest one?"

"*You* know," Alfie says, sounding sad. "Like, there's a funniest kid in every class, and a smartest kid, and a best jumper, and the one who's the cutest? It's just the name you get, EllWay," she explains.

"Oh. Yeah," I say. "The name you get. Kind of like with grown-ups, and what jobs they have. 'The teacher.' 'The doctor.' Stuff like that."

"I used to be the cutest," Alfie tells me, ignoring what I said about grown-ups' jobs. "But now, Suzette says I'm the meanest and *she's* the cutest."

"Suzette doesn't get to decide," I tell Alfie, trying to make her feel better.

"Yes she does," Alfie says. "Because the other kids do whatever she wants."

"That makes Suzette the bossiest, not the cutest," I say, laughing. "But don't tell *her* that, or you'll get sent home with another note for sure."

"Okay," Alfie says. "I won't tell her that. I'll think it, though. And I'll always get to be the cutest one at home, right?" she asks. "And you can be the cutest one's brother."

"Okay," I say, getting back to my game.

But later that night, when I think about what Alfie said, I think she's kind of right. Everybody is something.

But it's more than that. *Who* you are changes depending on *where* you are. Like here at home Alfie is everybody's "baby girl," and Mom is the lady who loves us all, no matter what we do, and Dad is the smart, strong guy who needs peace and quiet when he first gets home. He is also strict, but he loves us, too. A lot. And I'm the fun kid who likes to do stuff, and who only *sometimes* gets in trouble.

Everyone likes me at our house. I'm very popular here.

But at school, Jared and Stanley *don't* like me, at least some of the time, and neither do Cynthia and Heather—most of the time. At least I don't think they do.

At school, you don't get to choose the name you get, and you can't argue about it. It just *is*.

In the third grade at Oak Glen Primary School, Jared and Cynthia are usually the mean ones, like I said before, and Cynthia is also the bossy one, so she gets to be two things at school—both of them bad, in my opinion. But at home, Jared's mom and dad probably don't think he's mean. Maybe they think he's the quiet one in the family, or the hardest one to wake up in the morning, or something else. The point is, maybe he has a different name there.

I don't know *what* Cynthia's parents think. I feel sorry for them, that's all.

And to give you another example, Kry Rodriguez is the smartest kid in both math and spelling at school, but maybe at home she talks back to her parents or forgets to take out the trash. Probably not, but maybe.

At school, Fiona McNulty is the best artist, and she is also the shyest kid in the third grade—but maybe at home she's the funniest person in her family, or the loudest.

At school, my friend Corey is the kid who's the most afraid of math, especially mental math and standing-at-the-board math, but at home he's the champion swimmer who has to be fed exactly the right food to keep him in smooth operating condition. And he's brave during swim meets. He never cries. Some kids do, he told me once.

Those are just a few examples of what I'm talking about.

But what about me, when I'm at school? I

have always wanted to be the funniest kid in my class, the boy who other guys wanted to be friends with, since I can't be the **TALLEST** or the **STRONGEST**—which honestly would be my first choices, if I got to pick. But now, I'm starting to be known as the third-grade kid who messes up.

Like I said before, you don't get to choose.

Once you're away from home, stuff chooses you.

OCTOPUS TAG

I don't remember what April was like last year, it was so long ago. But this April has been very mixed-up in Oak Glen. Rainy, sunny, rainy, cloudy, windy, rainy, rainy.

And that's just in the past week!

It's like they put a little kid like Alfie in charge of the weather.

Today, Thursday, it rained all morning, but now the sun has come out and we get to have our afternoon recess outside.

FINALLY.

It seems like it has been days since we played outside, and our legs are jumpy. Also, the air in our classroom has been almost used up, in my opinion. What's left smells like floor cleaner, dry erase markers, pencil shavings, and old tuna sandwiches, all mixed up.

"Come *on*, EllRay," Corey says, his freckles looking like polka dots on his face, he is so excited. "We gotta grab a kick ball before they're all gone, for once."

"Yeah," Kevin says, with his usual serious look on his face. Kevin and I are alike in many ways. For example, we are the only black kids in our class, not counting two very quiet girls who are friends from church and who pretty much stick together. Kevin is a lot more careful and calm about things than I am, though. He never loses library books or forgets to get permission slips signed, and he has never had to go to the principal's office in his life. Not once.

But even though we hurry as fast as we can, Jared and Stanley reach the big net of kick balls first. Jared has rounded up all five of the balls like they're a bunch of red rubber eggs and he is the rooster in charge of guarding them.

"Sorry, losers," he shouts at us. "But we're practicing our kicking today, and we need all the balls." And his friend Stanley grins and gives us the thumbs-down sign with one of his

hands, and the loser sign on his forehead with the other—which you're not allowed to do at our school, but he does it anyway. And of course no one catches him. The playground monitor is way over at the other end of the playground. She is busy trying to talk on her cellphone and show a bunch of confused-looking first-graders how to play Capture the Flag at the same time, so *she* can't help us.

"Well, who even cares about kick balls?" Kevin shouts back, even though I know he does care, because he wanted to practice his kicking, too. I'm not sure why. Probably to improve his soccer skills.

"Yeah," I yell. "And anyway, we're gonna play Octopus Tag, and you can't!"

"Don't even want to." Jared's voice floats back over the heads of the jumping-rope girls, who are chanting *"Miss Mary Mack, Mack, Mack"* as they bounce up and down. Boys would get strangled if they tried that. But Jared sounds a little less sure of himself than before, because **OCTOPUS TAG** is our class's newest fun discovery.

I guess different people play it different ways, but here's how we play.

1. One person is the octopus, and the other kids stand far away in a line, and then they try to run past whoever the octopus is without getting tagged.

2. Whoever does get tagged has to sit or stand where they were tagged, and not move. Then they try to tag someone else when the kids run by the next time.

3. Pretty soon there are a whole bunch of kids helping

the octopus—they are his or her extra "arms"—
and they try to tag the kids who are left as they
run by.

4. And the kid who doesn't get tagged is the winner!

It's really fun, only the more kids the better.

"Who wants to be the octopus?" Kevin asks,
looking around.

"I do," Corey says, grinning. And so a bunch of
kids—including me—run to the other side of the
playground. Even some of the jumping-rope girls
join us, because this is a perfect day for Octopus
Tag. It's the kind of day when you could just keep
on running forever! The clouds are puffy and white,
like in cartoons, and the wind is blowing them
around. I think the wind is just as happy as we are.

Jared and Stanley watch us get ready to start
the game. I guess they're not having as much fun
hogging the kick balls as they thought they would,
since nobody else wants them.

"Okay, go!" Corey says, and we run toward him
screaming our heads off as we try to get past
without getting tagged. But Corey is a very good

athlete—he's the champion swimmer, remember—
and he tags two kids, Kevin and one of the church
friends.

By now, Stanley looks like he wishes he could
play Octopus Tag, too, but I think he's scared to
leave Jared-the-rooster standing there all alone.

The second time we run screaming across the
playground, Kevin almost tags me. He just barely
misses my arm, in fact. But Emma, Fiona, and another kid I don't know very well get tagged, so now
the octopus has lots of arms. Twelve, I think.

And I *do* get caught the
next time we run across the
playground—by Fiona, of all
people, who blushes when
she touches me and says,
"Sorry, EllRay."

Like I said before,
she's shy.

"That's okay," I say,
panting a little as I freeze
in place.

By now, there are only
a few kids left who haven't
been tagged, including
Cynthia, Heather, and
Kry. But all of a sudden
Jared and Stanley are
standing with them, get-
ting ready to run.

Oh. *Now* they want to play.

✳ **10** ✳

TUG-OF-WAR

"No fair," Kevin shouts to Jared and Stanley. He is still mad about them hogging the kick balls, I guess. "You can't start playing now, you guys. It's too late."

"That's right, you can't," I say, backing Kevin up. "Kids have already been tagged. You have to wait for the next game."

"Try and stop us, losers," Jared yells back. "We can play if we want to!"

"Yeah," Cynthia calls out, kissing up to Jared for no reason—except to be mean to me, maybe. "You're not the boss of the world, EllRay Jakes."

Like I want to be!

And **BOOM**. The kids who are left—*and* Jared and Stanley and his freckles—are running across the playground, trying to escape the octopus arms reaching out to tag them.

Stanley is the first one tagged, but Jared is

zigzagging back and forth like a champion football player. He's pretty far away from me, though.

It will be so not fair if he wins this game of Octopus Tag! I was the one who thought of it, and he cheated by not starting to play until it was almost over.

But here comes Cynthia, and she's heading straight toward me.

Cynthia, who said Zip was "only a goldfish."

Cynthia, who said she would never ask me to take care of *anything*.

Cynthia, who told everyone that I was the one who took home *Treasure Island*.

Cynthia, who just said, "You're not the boss of the world, EllRay Jakes."

And so I decide to stop Cynthia Harbison, no matter what.

I have to, to make things come out even.

All this thinking happens in about two seconds, and—*perfect*. Cynthia's not even looking at me, she's so worried about getting tagged by Emma

McGraw. So I reach toward Cynthia as if my arm has sudden elastic super-powers, and—*grab*.

"Gotcha," I shout, but Cynthia's not giving in without a fight, even though she's been tagged. She tries to pull away.

"You didn't get me," she says.

Doesn't she know the rules? I'm still touching her!

"**GOTCHA**," I say again, not letting go of her pink sweater sleeve, but she starts spinning around and around me. She is still not giving up.

"*Grrr*," she growls, baring her teeth and everything.

What is her problem?

"I won!" I hear Jared shout in the distance, and that just makes me angrier.

"You're *got*," I yell at Cynthia, still not letting go, because she really is the kind of person who might tell everyone that I didn't tag her at all. And that is not going to happen no matter *who* says he has already won.

There can't be two cheaters in one game, or what is the point of playing the game at all? Even one cheater ruins things!

By now, though, it's a tug-of-war between Cynthia and me over her sweater sleeve, which is stretching out with elastic super-powers of its own as we whirl around and around in a circle. "Let *go*," Cynthia says, gasping out the words. "You never tagged me, EllRay. I was winning!"

"I'm tagging you right now," I argue, dizzy and panting. "Hold still!"

"Let go!"

And all of a sudden I *do* let go, by accident, and she goes crashing onto the playground pavement.

"Owww," Cynthia cries, curling up into a ball,

and everyone comes running, including the playground monitor, of course—because Cynthia has become an instant sympathy magnet.

"Oh, you poor thing," some other girl says.

"Are you okay?"

"What *happened*?" kids are asking as the playground monitor quickly checks Cynthia over—for any cuts needing stitches, or broken bones, I guess.

But there is only a tiny bit of blood on one of Cynthia's knees. Just a speck or two, really. Not even specks. Dots is more like it.

"Aaack!" Cynthia screams, seeing the blood on her barely skinned knee. "EllRay wrecked me!"

"I did not," I say, trying to defend myself. "It was an accident! We were playing a game. And you were trying to **CHEAT**."

"You did *so* wreck

her," Heather Patton says, trying to show Cynthia how loyal she is. "Now she'll probably have a scab, and then a scar. And she was *perfect* before. Just perfect! And now she'll never be perfect again!"

"*Waaah*," Cynthia cries, hearing this.

I personally think that this is going a little far, saying that Cynthia Harbison used to be perfect, *ever*. But the kids standing around us seem so excited by this drama, and so grossed out by the microscopic blood on Cynthia's knee, that no one says anything to defend me.

Including Kevin, Corey, Emma, or Annie Pat.

And including me.

Because—what is there to say?

I messed up again.

✳ 11 ✳

YOU OWE ME!

"You two sit there," the playground monitor says to Cynthia and me, sounding both angry and worried as she points to two chairs outside the principal's office. The principal's door is open, but he's probably in the hallway, jumping out and saying *"Hi!"* to unsuspecting kids coming in from lunch. "Mrs. Tollefsen can slap a bandage on that knee for you when she gets back from the ladies room," the monitor tells Cynthia, talking about our school secretary. "The nurse isn't here on Thursdays."

It is obvious from the look on her face that Cynthia does not like this news about the missing school nurse one bit. "She's *not*?" she squawks. "But this could be serious!"

Yeah, right. A "serious" skinned knee with three tiny dots of blood on it. Okay, maybe four.

"I think you should call my mom," Cynthia says, tears filling her eyes again.

My dad calls this "turning on the waterworks" when Alfie does it.

"We'll let Mrs. Tollefsen decide about calling your mother," the playground monitor tells Cynthia, peeking at her watch. "I have to get to class. Do you think you two can control yourselves for a couple of minutes?"

"Yes," I mumble.

"I guess," Cynthia says, scootching her chair away from mine an inch or two—so she won't be infected by my badness. Or in case I start whirling her around again.

And all of a sudden we are alone.

Cynthia turns and stares at me. "You are in so much trouble, EllRay Jakes," she says. "Hitting a girl so hard that she falls over and bleeds."

WHAT?

"I didn't hit you, and you know it," I say, because somebody has to tell the truth around here. "Just saying stuff doesn't make it true, Cynthia. We were playing Octopus Tag. I tagged you, but you wouldn't stay tagged. That's all that happened."

"Nuh-uh," Cynthia says, shaking her head. "You went after me for no reason, and you hit me so hard that I fell on the ground. And *now* look at me," she says in a wobbly voice, pointing to her knee. "I'm wrecked, just like Heather said. And so is my poor, stretched-out pink sweater, which was brand-new last year. You *owe* me."

"You know it didn't happen like that, Cynthia," I say, trying to keep my own voice steady. "I never went after you. And I *had* to tag you. We were playing Octopus Tag! *That's why they call it tag.* You were running right at me. You didn't see me, that's all."

"Well, but you didn't have to hold onto my sweater the way you did," Cynthia says, petting its saggy sleeve like it's a little lost kitten.

"But you were gonna cheat," I argue. "You kept saying I never tagged you!"

"So what?" Cynthia says. "Making someone bleed is a lot worse than not playing some stupid game right, *EllRay*."

"I didn't make you bleed," I say. "You fell. It was an accident, and you know it."

"*They* won't know that," Cynthia says, her voice very loud and clear, and I can feel my heart slither down to my shoes, because—the grown-ups might believe her. *Everyone* might believe her sooner or later, even the kids who saw the real thing happen with their own eyes.

I'm starting to think that's the way things are in the world.

"*Who* won't know that it was an accident, Miss Harbison?" a man's voice asks, and Cynthia and I both look up.

It's the principal, and he's been in his office the whole time! And the door was open!

He heard *everything*.

Thankyouthankyouthankyouthankyou.

Cynthia jumps to her feet, even though no one told us yet that we could get up. "This bad boy was mean to me on the playground for no reason," she says, pointing her finger at me.

Okay. Cynthia knows the principal heard what she said, but she still thinks she might pull this off.

"Look," Cynthia says to the principal, showing him her skinned knee—as if it must be proof of *something*.

"Mrs. Tollefson will take care of that scrape in a minute or two," the principal says, barely giving Cynthia's knee a glance. "Why don't you two come into my office and sit down?"

This sounds like a question, but it isn't. So Cynthia and I don't make any suggestions of different activities to do. We follow the principal into his office.

I already know the way, unfortunately, but I think this is Cynthia's first time—unless she's been there to get a medal for being perfect or something.

No. She would have bragged to everyone if that had happened.

"Now, what's going on?" the principal asks, once we get settled into our uncomfortable chairs.

Cynthia and I look at each other for a second, and then, as if we have made a silent promise, we look away and try to erase our faces like marker boards. For once we share the same goal: to get out of the principal's office as fast as possible.

I mean, he's nice and everything, but he's the *principal.*

I just hope he doesn't call our parents, that's all. Being in trouble at school is bad enough, but being in trouble at home, too—at the same time? And for the same thing? That's just wrong!

"Nothing's going on," Cynthia mumbles.

"Everything's fine," I agree. "It was just an accident on the playground. It wasn't an *on-purpose.*"

"I'm glad to hear it," the principal says, staring at us through half-closed eyes as he pets his beard. "But I'm not too pleased about what I overheard you two saying out there."

Cynthia and I look at each other, then look away.

The principal doesn't say anything for one whole minute, which I know for sure because I count the seconds from one to sixty. And then he says, "Look. I'm not going to have any feuds going on here at Oak Glen. *Or* any roughhousing on the playground, *or* any fibbing about it afterward. Do you understand me?"

Cynthia gives me one of her old looks. "Do you understand him, EllRay?" she asks, sounding patient and forgiving at the same time.

If I could kick her "by accident," I really think I would.

"I was talking to both of you, Miss Harbison," the principal says, his voice sharp. "And I'll be keeping an eye on both of you. Understand that, please."

And Cynthia and I both nod our heads, because by now, we're too scared to say another word.

I can tell that Cynthia is furious, though, and

that she blames me—not herself—for this scold-
ing, on top of blaming me about her knee and her
stretched-out sweater.

But even though he's angry, the principal kind
of stuck up for me!

At least now, someone knows I'm not the *only*
kid here at Oak Glen who messes up.

For what that's worth.

✳ 12 ✳

CLASH

"You owe me, EllRay Jakes," Cynthia says again in a low voice as we walk down the hall toward our classroom holding our excuse slips. "You owe me big."

"I do not," I say. "This whole thing was an accident."

"Just look," Cynthia says, not even listening as she points to her knee. "Do these Band-Aids go with this outfit? No, they do not. I clash, and it's all your fault."

Cynthia now has two bright blue rocket ship Band-Aids on her barely scraped knee. "These are for kindergarten boys," Cynthia had objected to Mrs. Tollefson, but they were the only Band-Aids our school secretary could find. And Cynthia is almost angrier about those rocket ship Band-Aids than she was about getting knocked down at recess *or* being scolded by the principal.

"You have to make it up to me, EllRay, or else," Cynthia says as we get near our classroom. "You have to pay me back. It's, like, the law."

"Not if I didn't do anything wrong," I tell her, my hand on the sticky door handle. "Anyway, you don't get to decide stuff like that."

"Then the kids in our class will decide," she says, still keeping her voice low. "I'll tell them to vote on how bad you are. This is a democracy, don't forget."

"Oak Glen Primary School isn't really a democracy," I inform her. "They say it is, but we hardly get to vote on *anything*."

And it's true. We don't vote on anything important, like how much homework we get or how long recess should be. We just vote on stuff like should we sell magazine subscriptions, fancy popcorn, or chocolate bars for our fund-raiser.

"And anyway," I add, "a democracy is—well, it's voting for who's gonna be President. It's not kids voting on whether another kid did something wrong or not," I say, trying to come up with a good argument, fast. "The truth either happened or it didn't."

I just hope I'm right, that's all.

"Nope," Cynthia says, smoothing back her hair with one hand as she gets ready to push open the door with the other, even though I am still holding onto the handle. "There's gonna be a secret vote, and I'll run it. And then I'll tell you how it comes out. And if you lose, then you have to make it up to me about what happened at recess, and about the principal, and how you ruined my look with these stupid clashy Band-Aids. And I'll tell you *when* you have to do that, and *how*. Period."

"You can't just make rules and stuff up, Cynthia," I say. "You're not the boss of me," I add, sounding more like four-year-old Alfie than myself.

"Huh. Of course I am," Cynthia says, lifting her stuck-up chin high in the air. "Until you pay me back, anyway."

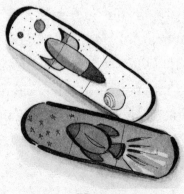

✳ **13** ✳

PLANNING MY GETAWAY

"Please open the milk, EllWay," Alfie says, staring hard at the find-the-mistakes cartoon on the back of her cereal box. "It's glued shut. How are we supposed to dwink it?"

"Okay," I say, prying open the container of milk and pushing it toward her. I barely look up from the comics I am reading.

Friday was full of Cynthia Harbison's scowls and whispers as she tried to get kids to vote on how bad I am, and how I "owe" her. But now it is Saturday morning, which means no school for two whole days.

Just in time, too. That was one rough week back there.

But Saturday mornings are always fun for Alfie and me. Mom and Dad sleep late, and Alfie and I are allowed to eat one big bowl of whatever cereal we want, even the kinds Mom won't let us eat any other day of the week. I'm in charge of pouring the milk. Then we get to watch cartoons or a DVD until ten o'clock, if we don't argue.

Alfie's cereal milk is pink this morning, and mine is kind of chocolate-y.

"Oh, guess what?" Alfie asks, looking up with a big smile on her face—and a line of pink milk crawling down her chin.

"What?" I say.

"Suzette's coming over to play today," Alfie says. "Yay!" she adds, I guess to show me how happy she is about this terrible news.

"Suzette *Monahan*?" I ask, almost dropping my spoon. "The same Suzette who threw torn-up paper in your hair and said you had to be the mean-est kid in day care from now on? Bossy Suzette?"

"Um-hmm," Alfie says, nodding. "Suzette's my friend again," she explains, still smiling big-time.

Mom hasn't fixed Alfie's hair for the day yet, so Alfie is still looking a little random, but cute—not that I'm going to tell her that. That's all she needs.

"I thought Suzette was mad at you," I say. "You know, for telling her she was gonna die some day and get buried in a plastic container in the back-yard."

"Or flushed down the toilet," Alfie adds, nodding again. "But she forgived me, because I apologized."

"What about you?" I ask, not bothering to correct her grammar, because what's the use? She's four. "Did you forgive *her*?"

"What for?" Alfie asks, after shoveling some more cereal into her mouth and thinking about my question.

"For saying that she got to be the cute one in day care now, and you had to be the mean one," I remind her.

"I decided to forget about that," Alfie tells me, like it never mattered in the first place. "Because I want to be Suzette's friend again more than I want to stay mad. So she's coming over. Yay!" she cheers again.

And what I want to know is this. Since when did Alfie become so forgiving? Like I have mentioned before, she is usually a very stubborn kid.

1. For example, Alfie got so mad at Mom once for not buying her this fancy doll at Target that she ran away to the front yard that afternoon. She even hung her favorite clothes on the fence using little white hangers.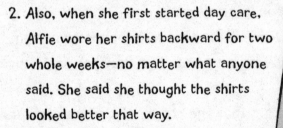

2. Also, when she first started day care, Alfie wore her shirts backward for two whole weeks—no matter what anyone said. She said she thought the shirts looked better that way.

3. And a few weeks ago, Dad got so fed up with Alfie about her picky eating that he said she had to finish her peas before she could leave the dinner table. Alfie sat there all alone after

dinner for more than one hour, gagging whenever she even looked at those peas. And she'd probably still be sitting there if I hadn't sneaked back into the dining room and eaten the whole pile of cold, wrinkled peas for her.

But Alfie can forgive terrible Suzette Monahan just like *that*? Suzette, who snooped around in my room while I was out the last time she came to play? I could tell! Suzette, who told my mom the last time she came over that she wanted McDonald's for her snack, not the oatmeal cookies Mom had just finished baking? Suzette, who has this thing about Alfie's hair—just because it's different from hers?

My sister's hair is lots prettier, by the way.

"Did Suzette at least apologize to you?" I ask Alfie, thinking about how hard it would be for me to forgive Cynthia, for instance. Unless Cynthia said she was sorry for making my life miserable, which she never would.

"Kind of," Alfie says. "She said I could be the *funny* girl in day care, instead of the mean girl. But she still gets to be the cute one."

"You're way cuter than she is," I inform my little sister. "And don't get stuck-up, but I'm not just saying that. What time is Suzette coming over?" I ask, scooping up another bite of cereal—and planning my getaway, because **NO WAY** am I going to be in this house when Suzette Monahan is here. I think I'm allergic to her, the way some kids are to peanuts.

"Before lunch," Alfie says, dribbling some more pink cereal milk down her chin. "Mommy's gonna go get her."

I hand Alfie a clean napkin. "Well, you guys have to stay out of my room this time," I tell her. "Because I'm going to be over at Corey's. Or Kevin's," I say, correcting myself when I remember that Corey probably has a swim meet this weekend—or, at the very least, practice. Swimming is the only thing Corey ever does in his spare time. I think his parents need him to be best at something. More than Corey needs to be the best, I mean.

"But me and Suzette were gonna make a pretend store in the backyard," Alfie says, her spoon drooping. "And I wanted you to come buy stuff, Ell-Way."

"I'll give you a quarter," I tell her fast. "And you can buy some things for me, okay? And put them outside my room. But pretend there's an invisible lock on the door."

"*Is* there?" Alfie asks, her eyes huge.

"Not really," I admit, because for some reason, I don't like to lie to my little sister. It's too easy, for one thing. What would be the point? "But pretend there's a lock, okay, Alfie? Because there's such a thing as privacy."

"Okay," Alfie says. "Hey," she says, looking at her imaginary wristwatch and smiling again, "it's almost time for our cartoons to start!"

"Yeah," I say. "Go turn on the TV, but not too loud. I'll rinse our bowls."

"Okay," Alfie says, and *POOF*. She's gone.

❄ **14** ❄

SUCH A STUPID FIGHT

The next Friday, just before lunch, we are supposed to be finishing up and turning in our *Treasure Island* art projects—which are supposed to be either maps of the island or pirate flags, but not just skulls and crossbones—while Ms. Sanchez takes some important papers to the office and talks with the principal. I am standing next to Ms. Sanchez's desk at the same time as Cynthia and Heather.

Almost everyone else in class has already handed in their maps and flags. They are now doing Sustained Silent Reading—or goofing around. But *silently*.

Cynthia slaps her fancy pirate flag onto Ms. Sanchez's desk. She did it on pink construction paper. It has palm trees and glitter coconuts on each side of the rainbow in the middle, and it doesn't look

very pirate-y to me. But maybe girl pirates love glitter and rainbows, I don't know.

Heather is holding the stars-and-stripes USA flag she made for the pirates. She is probably hoping that Ms. Sanchez will figure this project is so patriotic that she won't be able to say anything bad about it.

Heather likes to play things safe.

I made a map of what I think Treasure Island looks like, and it came out pretty good, in my opinion. I drew the Spy-glass hill and the North Inlet and the stockade. Everything. And I put pistols and knives all around the edges, which Mom helped me tear perfectly to make my map look old. I wanted to burn the edges a little, too, so it would look like my map was pulled out of a pirate ship fire, but Mom

said playing with fire was asking for trouble.

Listen. I will never need to *ask* for trouble, not when trouble seems to find me so easily.

Heather slides her flag under Cynthia's, but just as I put my map on top, Cynthia swats it away. "Mine gets to be on top," she whispers. "I want Ms. Sanchez to see it first. That's why I waited to turn it in. Duh."

"Watch *out*," I whisper back. "You almost ripped my map." I examine it carefully for damage.

"Oh, like you could *tell*," Cynthia says, laughing. And she nudges Heather until she laughs, too. "It's not like EllRay's map isn't already all ripped up," Cynthia says. "Look at it!"

"Yeah," Heather agrees. But I can tell she wishes

she weren't trapped in the middle of this.

"I tore the edges on purpose," I inform Cynthia.

All three of us are trying to keep our voices low, but a few kids—Emma, Annie Pat, and Kevin, especially—are looking up to see what's going on.

"It looks old, all right," Cynthia says, barely giving my excellent map a glance. "My palm tree flag goes on top, and that's final. I don't want my glitter coconuts getting all ruined."

And then she shoves me for no reason.

I stumble back a couple of steps, and two or three kids laugh. They sound a little nervous, but they laugh.

Okay. I know that a boy is never supposed to hit a girl, even when she's way bigger than he is, so I don't. But I nudge Cynthia with my shoulder when I try again to put my map on top of the pile of *Treasure Island* art projects.

"**OW**," Cynthia yells, clutching her arm like I just slugged it.

By now, everyone is watching us.

So much for Sustained Silent Reading. Now, it's Sustained Silent Staring.

"EllRay hit me," Cynthia announces to the class.

"He did not," Emma says, amazed. "We just saw the whole thing, Cynthia!"

"Yeah," Kevin, Corey, and Annie Pat agree, nodding their heads.

"Mind your own business," Cynthia tells them. She's really mad.

Cynthia turns her back to the class, and Heather crowds in close.

And I still haven't turned in my art project yet!

"I *am* putting my map on top of that pile, and you guys are not gonna stop me," I tell Cynthia and Heather.

"Put it under mine," Cynthia says.

"Why should I?" I ask.

"Just do it," Heather urges me, sounding nervous. "Just *do* it, EllRay. Please?"

And I am just about to shrug and give in, because this is such a stupid fight, when Cynthia shoves me again.

And so I shove her back.

Okay. One thing that I haven't mentioned yet is that right next to the pile of maps and flags is Ms. Sanchez's very important attendance notebook— and her water bottle, which she usually carries with her everywhere she goes for some reason. But she doesn't have it with her right now.

Inside her attendance notebook, Ms. Sanchez keeps very neat score each day of who is in class and who isn't. Then that becomes part of our permanent record. And it's written in secret code! She showed us once. For example, there are different marks for being in school, for being absent with no excuse, and for being absent with an excuse. And probably codes for other stuff, too, for all I know. Ms. Sanchez says the attendance notebook is her work of art.

We're not allowed to touch that notebook *ever*, it's so important.

"Quit shoving," Cynthia says, shoving me again.

"You quit shoving," I say, shoving her back.

"I'm gonna sock you one," Cynthia says.

She's going to *sock* me? Cynthia Harbison, whose hair and clothes and fingernails are always so tidy and clean? Cynthia, who likes to brag about her grades and her perfect record, and how dainty she is?

I don't *think* so!

If she actually does hit me, though, *I will not*

hit her back, I decide right then and there. But I will defend myself—and my pirate map—from her Fist of Doom, which is like the one in my video game *Die, Creature, Die*, only bigger.

I will figure out how to do this when the time comes.

"C'mon, Cynthia," Heather says, trying to pull her away from the desk. "Who cares if his stupid pirate map goes on top or not?"

"I care," Cynthia says, and she swings her straight arm toward me like it's a bat, and we're playing T-ball, and my head is the ball.

This is a dumb way to hit anything, which is probably why it doesn't work now, because I duck out of the way. But—over goes Ms. Sanchez's water bottle, right onto the famous secret code attendance notebook.

Frozen in horror, Cynthia, Heather, and I watch the water **GLUG, GLUG, GLUG** three times onto the very important notebook before any of us can move. But I'm the one who finally picks the bottle up—just as Ms. Sanchez walks in the door.

Naturally.

"Oh, no! Look what EllRay did, Ms. Sanchez,"

Cynthia cries out. "Your poor official attendance notebook! Your work of art! He threw water *all over it*. On purpose!"

"My notebook," Ms. Sanchez says, sprinting over to her desk, grabbing the notebook, and shaking it twice. She wipes the wet pages with the corner of her sweater.

"It's all EllRay's fault," Cynthia says, sounding almost scared.

"We'll discuss this later," Ms. Sanchez says, still dabbing at the notebook. "Later," she
says again, as if
she is too upset
to talk about it
right now.

✳ 15 ✳

BLAME IT ON ELLRAY

"Come over to the drinking fountain," Cynthia says a few minutes later, grabbing at my shirt in the crowded hallway when me and my friends are headed outside to eat lunch and play. "I have to talk to you."

"**TOUGH**," I say, yanking my arm away. "I never want to talk to you again, Cynthia Harbison. You liar."

"Yeah," Kevin says, scowling at Cynthia. "Liar. I don't think Ms. Sanchez even believed you when you tried to explain."

"C'mon, EllRay," Cynthia says, not looking at him. "It's important."

"So is telling the truth," I say. "Talk to me outside with my friends, if you have the guts."

"At the *boys'* table?" Cynthia says, like I just asked her to meet me inside the nearest garbage can.

"Yeah," I say. "If it's so important."

And to my surprise, Cynthia—and her robot friend Heather, of course—follow us outside.

✕ ✕ ✕

At Oak Glen Primary School, kids can eat their lunch in the school cafeteria whether they buy lunch or not, or they can eat outside on the picnic tables, which is a lot more fun. The different grades eat lunch at different times, so we third graders get two tables all to ourselves, one for the boys and one for the girls.

The tables are on the grass, near two big trees you aren't allowed to climb.

I sit down at the boys' table next to Kevin and across from Corey. Jared and Stanley are already stuffing their faces, those luckies.

And Cynthia actually walks up to me and tugs my shirt again. "This will just take a minute," she whispers, almost polite—because she is on the boys' property, I guess.

I can tell that none of the boys likes having a girl so nearby, so I very s-l-o-w-l-y get up and follow Cynthia to one of the trees. "Go away," I tell Heather, who is trailing after Cynthia like a shadow. "Or else my friends get to listen in, too. Two against one is no fair."

And so Heather looks at Cynthia—for permission to leave, I guess—and then melts away to the girls' picnic table, where Fiona, Kry, and the two church friends are already giggling and eating their lunch.

Girls cannot eat without giggling, by the way. It's a fact.

Cynthia takes off her plastic headband in a serious way, tosses her straight hair, then scrapes the headband back on over it. It's like she needs everything to be perfect before she can even start talking. "Listen," she tells me. "I'm sorry if I got you in trouble for spilling Ms. Sanchez's water bottle."

"Well, maybe you didn't get me in trouble," I say. "Ms. Sanchez says that even though the pages are curly now, everything was written in permanent ink. And she hasn't yelled at me yet. And I *didn't* spill the water bottle, in case you forgot. *You* did, when you tried to sock me." I have to keep reminding her, because Cynthia Harbison is exactly the

kind of person who believes that saying something
two or three times makes it the truth.

I have the feeling you have to watch it with
people like that.

"Yeah, but that's my point," Cynthia says, like
she's just won the argument. "Ms. Sanchez doesn't
even care, *because* of the permanent ink."

"She cares," I argue. "The water glugged all over
her work of art. And it even soaked into some of the
art projects."

"Not mine," Cynthia says, shrugging. "Because
mine was on top." She gets a look on her face like

it's hard getting through to me, I'm so dumb. "I mean, she won't care if *you* did it, EllRay. Because she's so used to you messing up."

"But I didn't mess up!" I shout. "And I'm gonna tell Ms. Sanchez what really happened when she asks," I add, trying to lower my voice.

And I start to go back to the boys' lunch table, because—what is the point of arguing with someone like Cynthia Harbison? It's a waste of your brain!

"No, wait," Cynthia calls after me. "Listen," she says again, catching up. "*You owe me.* Remember? Recess? And going to the principal? And the rocket ship Band-Aids? So when the water bottle accidentally spilled for no reason, I thought, 'I should just blame it on EllRay. Then we'll be even.' Think about it, EllRay. It's a great idea," she says, her voice suddenly soft as she tries to convince me.

And she pauses a minute, letting the brilliance of her "great idea" sink in.

She actually looks hopeful, like she needs this to happen.

Huh?

✳ 16 ✳

MAYBE

"Well, number one," I tell Cynthia, my voice as cold as an ice cube, "I don't owe you anything. And number two, why should I take the blame for something you did?"

"Because it doesn't matter for *you*," she says, like she's eager to explain. "You're already the kid in our class who messes up, and I'm already the kid who has the perfect record. So all I'm asking is that you take this *teensy-weensy blame* for spilling Ms. Sanchez's water bottle, and we'll be even about recess and the principal and the clashy Band-Aids. You won't owe me anymore. I mean, it *could* have been you who knocked the water bottle over, right?"

"Wrong," I tell her. "I wasn't the one swinging my Fist of Doom through the air for no reason,

Cynthia. I was just trying to turn in my *Treasure Island* map, that's all."

"And I was trying to help," she says, lying again. "It was an accident."

"Maybe," I say. "But you caused it."

"*Listen*," Cynthia says for the third time, like she really needs to tell me something. "You don't understand. I just *can't* get in trouble with Ms. Sanchez, EllRay. You're used to it, but I'm not."

Cynthia's probably right about one thing, even though Ms. Sanchez is my teacher, too. I guess I *am* getting used to being in trouble, not that I ever planned for my life to turn out this way. But before I can think up an actual reply, there is a tap on my shoulder.

It's Emma McGraw.

"Ms. Sanchez says she wants to see you in the classroom, EllRay," Emma tells me, not looking at Cynthia. "Right away."

"But I didn't get to eat yet," I say, thinking of the big sandwich I helped my mom make this morning. It has turkey bologna on it, and pickles, and no mustard, and everything. "I'm gonna *starve*."

No wonder I'm the littlest kid in our class!

"She says you can bring your lunch with you," Emma says, still not looking at Cynthia, who is giving her the **STINK-EYE**.

"Oh, *okay*," I say, and I stomp off to the boys' picnic table to get it.

That sandwich had better still be in my lunch sack, that's all I'm saying.

✕ ✕ ✕

"Have a seat, Mr. Jakes," Ms. Sanchez says, looking friendlier than I thought she would, considering.

"Okay," I say cautiously, and I sit down in the chair she has pulled up next to her desk. But I don't open my lunch sack, because I don't want to have turkey bologna flapping in my mouth when my teacher starts asking me complicated questions.

"So, what happened this morning?" Ms. Sanchez asks.

"Well, I got up," I say, stalling. "And then I took a shower, and—"

"EllRay," Ms. Sanchez interrupts. "You know what I mean."

"Okay," I say again. But I don't blab the truth right away, because I'm thinking.

1. Maybe Cynthia's right.
2. Maybe I *should* take the blame for knocking over that water bottle.
3. After all, Cynthia needs to be perfect, and it's already w-a-a-a-y too late for that for me, even if we're just talking about the last couple of weeks.
4. So what difference would it make to me if I took the blame?
5. Maybe I'm already doomed!

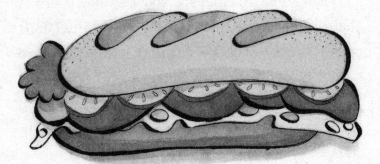

✴ **17** ✴

THE GEODE

"EllRay?" Ms. Sanchez says, reminding me that she is still waiting for an answer.

"Sorry," I mumble, and I get ready to walk the plank.

That's right. Suddenly I just want to get it over with. I will walk to the end of the plank, take a deep, deep breath, then drop off into the cold dark ocean.

It feels like I don't even have a choice.

"I guess spilling your water bottle was all my fault," I say to Ms. Sanchez. "I guess I kind of waved my arms around at Cynthia and Heather, and—"

"Stop right there," Ms. Sanchez says, holding up her hand. "I must tell you that I heard from another source that the whole unfortunate episode happened in quite a different way."

Whoa. Fancy words alert. Somebody blabbed?

Emma?

"And I'm not even talking about my soggy attendance notebook anymore," Ms. Sanchez says. "Why
are you so willing to take the blame, sweetie?" she
asks, her voice gentle. "That's the question."

Ga-a-ack! This is the second time this semester
that Ms. Sanchez has called me "sweetie"! Well, at
least there are no other kids in the room this time.

"Why, EllRay?" Ms. Sanchez asks again.

And I can't think of anything to say, because it's
too hard to explain.

Or maybe I can't think because I'm starving.
Even my *brain* is empty.

"Look," Ms. Sanchez says, pointing toward Zip's
still-empty fish bowl, which is sitting on the table
behind her desk. "Do you see that?"

"You don't have to remind me," I say, wondering
when she is gonna take it home, for pete's sake.

"Do you see the geode?" she asks, being more
exact this time. "That's you, EllRay Jakes."

Huh? Gee, thanks a lot!

"I'm a *rock*?" I manage to ask.

"I mean, if people were rocks, I'd say you were
that geode," she explains. "A little rough on the out-

side, at least lately, but beautiful and precious on the inside."

Beautiful and precious? And I thought "sweetie" was bad!

"Please don't tell that to the kids, okay?" I say, mumbling again.

But Ms. Sanchez just laughs. "Being beautiful on the inside is *much* better than being rough and hard all the way through, the way some people seem to be. At least lately," she points out.

"It's not as good as being a *crystal* all the way through, though," I say.

"Well, not many people are as good as that," Ms. Sanchez tells me. "Only a very few, in fact."

Ms. Sanchez is one of them, I think—but of course I could never tell *her* that. She'd think I was kissing up to her. *Smo-o-o-ch.*

YUCK!

"I want you to listen to me, EllRay Jakes," Ms. Sanchez says, leaning forward. "Your reputation is your most precious possession. You have to protect it. You must fight for it. You cannot surrender it so easily, whatever the reason."

"But I don't *have* a good reputation," I blurt out. "Not anymore. Not since the dead fish thing, and the book I forgot to bring back. Not to mention sometimes getting in trouble for bothering my neighbor during Sustained Silent Reading, and forgetting to get official permission slips signed, and stuff like that. I'm getting *famous* for messing up."

"I'm not saying there isn't room for improvement," Ms. Sanchez admits, uttering those dreaded words. "But I *am* saying you're a wonderful boy all the same. Just don't give up on yourself, EllRay. I have great hopes for you, and so do your mom and dad."

"Okay," I say, sneaking a look at the wall clock and hoping Ms. Sanchez isn't going to ask me again who spilled the water—because now, I'm still not sure what I'd tell her.

Grown-ups don't know how hard it is sometimes to be a kid.

Also, I am hoping there is still time for me to eat my sandwich, because my stomach is actually *growling*—the way Cynthia did on the playground that day. "May I please be excused?" I ask, as if Ms. Sanchez is my mom, and we're sitting at the dinner table.

"Yes," Ms. Sanchez says. "You certainly may. But I'm going to make an announcement at the end of class today."

"What kind of announcement?" I ask, my heart suddenly bouncing around in my skinny chest like a marble in a shoebox.

"Wait and see," Ms. Sanchez says.

✳ 18 ✳

PERSONAL BEST

"And now," Ms. Sanchez says later that afternoon, about twenty minutes before school is over for the week, "we have a few items of business to take care of. First, I'll ask Annie Pat and Corey to hand out the latest progress reports for you to take home and get signed. I'd like them back first thing Monday morning, ladies and gentlemen."

The progress reports are in licked-shut envelopes, of course, with our names printed in big letters on the front.

I am going to remember to get that thing signed by Monday, I promise myself. No matter *what* it might say inside! I want to show Ms. Sanchez that I can do it.

"Silence, please," Ms. Sanchez says when the progress reports have all been handed out. "Next, there's an announcement I'd like to make."

Cynthia sits up straight in her chair and folds her hands on the desk in front of her like she's getting ready to hear me get all the blame for spilling that water.

Ms. Sanchez is about to tell everyone how beautiful and precious I am, I think, horrified. "No, wait!" I hear myself say.

Ms. Sanchez stares at me. "You'd like to say something?" she finally asks.

"I guess," I say, and I walk with concrete feet to the front of the class. "Hi," I tell everyone. "My announcement is about this hand-held video game I like to play. It's called *Die, Creature, Die.*"

A couple of girls in my class look instantly bored, like they were just touched with a magic wand, and Cynthia looks confused. But most of the boys are surprised and excited to hear me talking about this game. They like it, too.

Ms. Sanchez just looks surprised. "**TICK-TOCK**, EllRay," she says, which is Ms.-Sanchez-speak for "*Hurry up.*"

"So, I really like this game," I tell everyone again, speeding up a little. "Only I'm not very good at it. Not like Stanley and Kevin, anyway."

Stanley and Kevin sit up straighter in their chairs and try to look modest.

"In fact, I'm almost terrible at it," I say. "But *Die, Creature, Die* is the newest game I have, and it's really fun to play. And my 'personal best' is getting better, and that's what this announcement is about."

Ms. Sanchez relaxes a little, but most of the rest of the kids in class just look confused.

"*Big deal*," Cynthia cough-says into her hand.

"In case you didn't know," I say, talking over her, "'personal best' means how much you improve at something, competing only against yourself. And improving takes time. You have to keep working at stuff to get better. You have to keep on trying, no matter how bad things look."

"Very good, EllRay," Ms. Sanchez says in a quiet voice as she beams at me.

"And another thing," I add, before she can call me sweetie again, or suggest that I sit down, "is that nobody can take your personal best away from you. Not if you don't let them. Like, if someone else is having trouble with *their* game, well I'm sorry, but that's their problem. No matter how perfect they usually are."

Cynthia Harbison slides down low in her chair.

"The end," I say, because I can't think of how else to finish my speech.

And I walk back to my chair—on bouncier feet this time.

A few of the kids in my class wriggle in their seats, as if they are silently saying, *"Huh? What was that about?"*

But a couple of kids have figured it out.

"Well, *I* have an announcement to make, too," Ms. Sanchez says. "It's about a certain young man I know. Now, this young man happens to be such a gentleman that when his four-year-old sister accidentally killed someone else's pet fish, he took the blame for it, regardless of how bad that made him look."

There is another wriggle in our class, and the kids look at the empty fish bowl as if they expect Zip magically to reappear and take a final bow. Maybe with little wings and a halo like a cartoon angel, I don't know.

"And yes," Ms. Sanchez continues, still not looking at anyone in particular. "This young man may
once have forgotten to bring a book he borrowed
back to class, but nobody's perfect, are they?"

Cynthia clamps her lips shut until they are just
a skinny pink line. You can tell this is not *her* favorite saying.

"But this particular young man had a lot on his
mind that day," Ms. Sanchez is saying. "And, may I
mention, he obviously loved that book. Why, he finished the entire thing during spring break! I could
tell that by looking at the very fine map he drew."

Now *I'm* the one sinking down in my chair, because she is talking about *Treasure Island.* And
my map. And me.

"This is also a very loyal young man, ladies and
gentlemen," Ms. Sanchez continues as my cheeks
get hotter. "He doesn't blame others when he makes
a mistake. He is a valued member of this classroom
community. And as far as the principal and I are
concerned, his reputation is spotless."

The principal! Spotless!

"And now," Ms. Sanchez says, "because this is

a democracy, I'd like for you all to elect a member of this class to go out and buy our next class mascot with this money." And she gets a five dollar bill out of her purse. "But it has to be a goldfish," she adds quickly, seeing the gleam in a few kids' eyes as they are obviously thinking, *"Rat!" "Tarantula!" "Bright green snake!"*

Emma raises her hand. "I nominate EllRay Jakes to buy our class's official new fish," she says when Ms. Sanchez calls on her.

This is really nice of Emma, considering that Annie Pat, Emma's best friend, wants to be the marine biologist—a fish expert—when she grows up, like I said before. But Annie Pat doesn't even look mad.

Kevin's and Corey's hands go up at the same time. "I second the nomination," Corey says, after Ms. Sanchez calls his name.

"Are there any other nominations?" Ms. Sanchez asks.

Heather Patton looks at Cynthia, as if asking whether or not Cynthia wants to compete against me for this honor, but Cynthia has just about disappeared, she has slumped so low in her chair.

She's staring straight ahead—at nothing. But perfectly, of course.

I actually feel sorry for her.

"Then we'll vote," Ms. Sanchez says, glancing at the wall clock to see how much time we have left. "All in favor of EllRay Jakes selecting our next goldfish this weekend say '**AYE**.'"

And a ragged chorus of "ayes" floats around the room.

"Opposed?" Ms. Sanchez asks, and I wait for the "nays" to boom out.

Only there aren't any.

Cynthia and Heather may be *thinking* "nay," but that doesn't count.

"Then EllRay it is," Ms. Sanchez says, smiling as she hands me the five dollars. "Don't you lose that, mister," she whispers so softly that only I can hear.

"I won't," I whisper back, smiling so wide that it feels like my ears might fall off. This is the first time I have ever won an election! It feels *good*.

The end-of-school buzzer sounds, and, too late, Annie Pat claps her hands over her sensitive pink ears.

"Get those progress reports signed this week-end, people," Ms. Sanchez calls out over the uproar that is us, getting ready to escape Oak Glen Primary School for a beautiful and precious weekend.

"Okay," a couple of dutiful kids call out.

But me and my friends are already halfway out the door—and on to the next fun thing.

I *am* going to remember to get that progress report signed, though.

And I won't lose Ms. Sanchez's five dollars, no matter what.

And I'll buy our class the best official new fish possible.

People are counting on me!

HAVE MORE FUN WITH ELLRAY IN

EllRay Jakes
is a Rock Star!

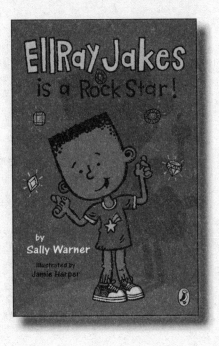

The second book in the EllRay series

by Sally Warner and Jamie Harper

THE FUN CONTINUES IN

EllRay Jakes
the Dragon Slayer!

The third book in the EllRay series
by Sally Warner and Jamie Harper